DE LOVE UNDER CONSTRUCTION

FLORA NY

THIS BOOK IS DEDICATED TO GOD ALMIGHTY AND MY FAMILY

CONTENTS

PROLOGUE

A short little tale of a man who finds love in an unexpected fashion. This is not a stroke story if thats what you're expecting , pass this one.
Its slow to start but he gets where he needs to be. Its a slice out of a person's life.

CHAPTER 1

When I bought my new house, I figured I would have the time to mow the yard and do all the things that a new homeowner does. Unfortunately, it didn't work out that way. I didn't buy some huge mansion with acres of yard to take care of. I searched around for a while before I decided on the neighborhood and the house. It was an out of the way subdivision, right on the edge of town. It was quiet because the access street was a dead end, so there wasn't any through traffic to worry about.

I picked an empty lot that had tons of trees on it and contracted it out to have something really nice built. I specified a few details with the architect and the price was agreed on. Eight months later I had my house, although I had to finish it myself. I had rented an apartment while the construction was going on and I frequently made myself an annoyance to the general contractor, until I fired him, that is. They hated to see me show up. My thoughts on that were simple, don't try to fuck me over with cheap shit when I paid for the good stuff and we'll get along just fine.

I eventually had to take the guy to small claims court over some fixtures that were specified in the blueprints but he had tried to substitute them with cheap knock-offs. It went on constantly; I caught the electrician trying to install Romex when the blueprints said conduit and solid #12 copper wires. He tried to switch the nameplates on a cheap GE main panel box when I specified a Square D commercial grade instead.

During my many trips out to the job site I would see the school bus drive by and drop off the high school kids at the corner. The first few times I ignored this and paid attention to the crooked bastards that were building my home. Just before school was going to be out for the summer, I started to pay attention a little more. Don't get me wrong, I'm not a pervert, I was looking for the kids that would be trouble once the daily babysitting was over.

I remembered what I had done as a teenager when a job site was available to plunder at night after all the workers went home. So I was looking for the kids that would do the same thing. I knew I'd recognize the look when I saw it. That calculating stare that said the brain behind the eyes was planning something not altogether kosher. What came as a complete surprise was the fact that it wasn't a boy that I caught looking over at the job site like that, it was a girl.

She was dressed about the same as the others but she was always off by herself, walking behind the others. None of the other kids talked to her or even paid that much attention to her. Her medium length black hair always covered most of her face as she walked along the street towards her house. I had ignored her like the rest of the kids did and it was by pure accident that I managed to see her looking over in my direction.

I was yelling at the contractor again because I had spotted the fake European bathroom fixtures in the back of his pick-up and had torn into him for trying to cheat me out of what I had paid for. My back had been to the street and before the argument escalated to violence, I spun around and walked over to my car to grab the cell phone. I was planning to call my lawyer again and see about what it would take to get an honest contractor in this town.

I had just placed the call when the kids went walking by and I caught her looking right at me. Her dark, almond shaped eyes were taking in everything, like she was memorizing every detail. This caught my attention and I turned to look at her and then the look was gone. She went back to hiding behind that shiny black hair. I muttered an apology to my lawyer's secretary and went on to explain why I called this time.

Due to the unions having everything locked up I couldn't get an honest contractor. I had to do something because nothing was getting done and I hated losing money to those crooked bastards. After working some details out with my lawyer, I decided to finish the house by myself with some general laborers. I hired a private security company to keep an eye on the place at night.

Two weeks went by with me getting very little sleep from all the sore muscles and planning out the next day's work schedule. I had to do a lot of remembering from my days in high school shop to complete the work. I picked up a hardcover NEC (National Electrical Code) book to help me with the electrical work. The general labor I managed to find weren't the smartest guys in the business, but they did work hard for the seventy-five bucks a day I was paying them.

Since I was so busy keeping the laborers busy and doing some of the more complicated work myself, I didn't have an opportunity to keep an eye on the neighborhood kids. However, one day I was up on the roof doing the final wiring on the attic exhaust fan when I spotted the dark haired girl watching me. She was sitting in the shade under a rather large willow tree across the street. Her back was against the trunk and she was reading a book, or at least she was pretending to.

I was under the roof attaching the last coupling on the conduit run into the junction box when I spotted her. She had the book up on her knees but her eyes were on me. When I poked my head up out of the hole and looked towards her. Our eyes met for a brief moment, and then she looked down at her book. I thought to myself that she was really cute and I wouldn't mind having her stare at me some more.

That stopped me for a moment when I realized I was thinking those kinds of thoughts about a girl that was in high school. It was obvious I wasn't the only one who thought she was cute because I noticed that the guys were giving her some attention too. She didn't return their stares like she did mine. She ignored them and only seemed to pay attention to me. Interesting.

After being up in the attic area for two hours I was dizzy from the heat. I decided that I'd leave the rest of the work until tomorrow morning when it would be cooler. I'd had enough for today and I wanted a bit of peace. So I told the crew to knock off for the day. I went over to the water spigot and after the hot water was cleared from the hose, I washed my face. I felt instant relief as the cold water raced down the back of my neck. I soaked my shirt and pants but I didn't care, the cold water felt invigorating. I drank from the hose before shutting it off.

That was a mistake. I had been so thirsty that I drank until I was full. Now I had a stomachache and my head felt like it was full of cotton. My legs felt rubbery. I didn't think I could stand up for much longer. I staggered over to the shade and plopped down against the side of the house. That's the last thing I remember.

When coming awake I felt a soft hand stroke my cheek. I groaned and tasted bile in my mouth. When I opened my eyes and looked around there was no one there. Strange, I thought. Well, I had obviously suffered a minor heat stroke and the touch could have been a form of hallucination. I slowly sat up trying to figure out if I was going to be okay. I had puked while I had been unconscious and I could feel that awful gritty sensation on my teeth.

I stood up, feeling a little unsteady, but I managed not to fall over. I went over to the spigot and rinsed out my mouth. My shirt was a mess and I stripped it off. I gave myself a quick shower standing there in my yard, not caring if anyone saw me. I wasn't about to take my pants off in public. I washed them off as best I could. I didn't want to take the chance of driving while feeling this crappy. I wobbled back over to the shade. That's when I noticed the small footprints in the dirt.

So, the touch on my cheek hadn't been a hallucination. Even more interesting, I thought. Did that mean she liked me? Or was it simply a case of her being a Good Samaritan? What did I want it to be? The safe thing would be the latter but a small part of me wanted it to be the former. I leaned against the side of the house and looked around again. Movement caught my eye and I pretended not to notice. Someone was hiding around the corner of the house next door.

I stared at a point down the street and waited to see if the person hiding would peek out again while my head was turned. Sure enough, a few seconds later a patch of dark hair appeared and one eye looked in my direction. Again, I pretended not to notice and continued to stare down the street. I decided that if she wanted to look, I'd give her something to look at. I stretched out my arms and arched my back. I slowly twisted side-to-side and popped my back and loosened up a bit. That did feel good. I rolled my shoulders and leaned back against the house.

The entire time I did this, I had watched her in my peripheral vision. She had poked her head out completely and her eyes missed nothing while I stretched. I couldn't help grinning while I did this. I think she finally saw the grin and her head disappeared behind the house again. I chuckled to myself and realized I felt pretty good. I stood up and stretched again. That was a mistake. My vision blurred and spots danced in my eyes. Whoa. That's not good.

The dizziness didn't go away and I suddenly found myself on my knees. I caught myself on my hands before planting my face in the dirt. The urge to heave up the water in my stomach briefly washed over me and I fought it off. I felt a pair of hands touch my shoulders and I slowly turned my head to look. The girl had come over and was kneeling next to me and looking at me with concern on her face. I gave her a small smile of thanks and grunted.

She blushed when I smiled at her. A tiny, high-pitched voice asked,

"Are you okay, mister?"

I nodded but didn't say anything. That voice sounded like it came from a little girl, not a mature teenager. She backed away a couple steps when I sat back on my heels. I massaged the back of my neck and tried to gather my wits. Out of the corner of my eye, I watched her bring her hands up and she sniffed her fingers. My first thought was that I had missed something when I had washed off earlier. A tiny smile formed on her face as she sniffed her fingers.

That action dashed any notion that I had about missing a spot. She caught my strange look, blushing furiously; she dropped her hands. For a few seconds, she seemed unsure of what to do or where to look. I tried to be a gentleman about the whole episode and pretended not to care about her actions.

Coughing and clearing my throat, I tried to think of what to say. It was odd; I hadn't felt this unsure of myself in a long time.

"Uhm... thanks for looking out for me."

Her blush returned and she nodded, but kept silent. She had one foot idly making small circles in the dirt and her head bowed, looking at me through her bangs. I was frozen in time, looking at this cutie. A very strange feeling washed over me while I looked at her. There was helium in my brain and lead in my feet. This had never happened to me before. I tried to convince myself that it was due to my heat stress. But I was lying to myself at this point. It was her. All her.

I couldn't breathe. I watched her every move. She grinned at my reaction. I wanted to take her right there in the yard. Right in front of god and everyone. I didn't care what anybody thought. I suddenly remembered my manners and shook my head to clear out the fog of lust that filled me.

"What's your name, angel?"

I didn't think it was possible, but her blush darkened even further.

"Li Yung Quang."

The high lilt and singsong cadence of her response sounded strange to my ears. She giggled at what must have been a very odd expression on my face.

"Lie Young Qwahaung?" I tried to repeat. This brought on a fit of giggles and she shook her head.

"No. Just call me Sunshine. Everyone else does."

"Okay, sorry I messed up trying to pronounce your name. I've never heard anything like it before. When you say it, it sounds beautiful. But I'm afraid my thick skull and fumbling tongue can't get it right."

She smiled at my self-depreciation. I lost myself in her smile for a moment and realized that she was waiting for me to tell her my name.

"Oh, um, sorry. Forgot my manners for a second. I'm Peter Branhagen."

"Peter Branhagen. That's a nice name."

"It is when you say it like that."

My comment made her blush. She seemed to shrink into herself for a moment. A very lusty thought flashed through my mind but I quickly dismissed it. I didn't want to frighten her away now that I had her talking to me. She seemed rather perceptive. Of course, I'm also not very good about hiding what I'm thinking either.

"Sorry, I wasn't making fun of you. I mean it. You have a beautiful voice and I like hearing it. It matches the rest of you."

I watched as she thought about what I said. The genuine smile that spread across her face sent those funny sensations through me again. Her jaw moved back and forth with her tongue pushing out her cheek. Oh god. I think I'm in lust. Whoa. I'd better get a hold of myself before I do something really stupid. She's in high school. I'm not. I am so not supposed to be looking at her with these thoughts.

I think she saw the guilt and conflict on my face. She looked around quickly to see if we had an audience. I stopped myself from doing the same. No sense in looking totally obvious. She gave me a quick nod.

"I'd better get home now. Maybe I'll see you around some other time."

With that, she left. I tried not to bore holes in her cute wiggling butt. I failed. Oh damn. What am I going to do now? I looked away before she could catch me staring. I put my hand against the side of the house and pushed myself up. I got the spare emergency blanket out and put it over the seat in my truck. Now I wouldn't have a wet seat going back to my apartment.

Later that evening I was sitting in my comfy chair slowly sipping on a beer. I had showered and was now trying to recover from my earlier stupidity. I rubbed my stiff one through my boxer briefs while thinking about her ass. I tried not to obsess over it but I couldn't help it. It was perfect according to the Pete scale, and 'little Pete' thought it was even better than that.

I tried to rationalize my feelings for such a young girl. The thing was, she had been watching me for several weeks. Granted, at first I thought that she was scoping out the place for mischief, but now I knew she had been watching me. So what does this mean? Could I have a relationship with this girl? Hmmm. I had no easy answers for these questions. Finishing my beer, I tossed the empty into the trash and went to bed.

The following morning I packed some extra Gatorade in my cooler. As fond as I was of having Sunshine being near me, I didn't need a repeat of yesterday. Sunshine. Yeah, she was that all right. I spent the morning finishing up the attic work before it became a blast furnace. When I took a break at mid-morning, I casually glanced around the neighborhood. I didn't spot my dark-haired angel. Perhaps she was hiding especially well.

The thought that I might have frightened her off last night slowly occurred to me. Damn. I shrugged and went back to work. When it was lunchtime the gang loaded up in their vehicles and went on a burger run. Since I had brought my lunch today, I stayed behind to keep an eye on the place. I rolled an empty cable spool over to the porch to put my feet on while I relaxed. I ate my egg salad sandwich and pretzels in peace. I opened up my 'special' cooler that had several cans of soda floating in brine water and ice. I rinsed off the brine and popped one open. Ahhhhhh, nothing beats a Dr. Pepper slushy on a hot day!

I was stupid. I chugged it. Brain freeze! Ugh. While I squeezed my eyes shut against the sudden ache, I heard someone snickering. I opened my eyes and found my angel of mercy standing in front of me. Her grin was so cute!

"What's the matter, Peter? Got a headache?"

"Yeah. I drank my Dr. Pepper slushy too fast."

"Dr. Pepper slushy? Where'd you get one of those?"

"I made it myself. Would you like one?"

She blushed and nodded. I got off the cooler and fished out another can.

"Rinse off the can before you open it. There's salt water residue all over it."

"Oh, so that's how you got them so cold. Neat."

After she rinsed off her can, she walked back over to me and sipped hers. I grinned.

"Not going to chug yours?"

"Nope. I don't need to induce any dain bramage."

"Hah! Good one. Funny and beautiful, a winning combination."

She blushed and hid behind her bangs again. Although it was cute the first couple of times, I was getting a little tired of trying to look at her face through that veil. I decided I was going to do something about it.

"Sunshine, do me a favor. Please don't hide your beauty behind your hair."

She slowly looked up at me. She almost hid her smile.

"You think I'm beautiful?"

I almost screwed up. Almost. I kept my smartass answer in check.

"Yes, I do. I like losing myself into those dark eyes of yours and I definitely bask in the warmth of your smile."

Shit. Where'd that cheesy line come from? If I had said something like that to one of the women at the singles bar I would have gotten nothing less than a derisive sneer. However, to a teenage girl, it was poetry. She got a dreamy look on her face and blushed again. This time she made the effort and looked right at me.

"Much better, Sunshine. Thank you."

I dropped my feet off the cable spool and she sat down. I flipped open my lunch box and retrieved the last item, a sack of chewy chocolate chip cookies. Sunshine's eyes lit up and she smiled when I offered her one.

"Thank you. These are my favorites."

I nodded in agreement and stuffed one in my mouth. We both hummed while we chewed. We grinned at each other at our reaction to the soft chewy goodness of the cookies. A slightly uncomfortable silence settled between us. I wasn't sure what to say or do from here. I was mildly attracted to her but just couldn't bring myself to cross that line yet. She seemed to sense my unease.

"Thanks for the slushy and the cookies. I gotta go now. See ya later, Peter."

"Um, okay, Sunshine."

I watched her walk away and couldn't help myself—I stared at her wiggling rear end. Very nice. Just as she reached the sidewalk, she glanced over her shoulder back at me. I wasn't fast enough; she caught me staring. It was my turn to blush. She gave me a quick grin and continued down the street.

The crew returned from their lunch and I got back to work. I couldn't stop thinking about that little grin she gave me. She knew I had been staring at her butt and she didn't mind. I really needed to concentrate on my work and what the others were doing. I pushed those thoughts about her butt aside.

Sunshine visited me during my lunch break every day for the rest of the week. We shared chewy chocolate chip cookies and Dr. Pepper slushies. She was very curious about me. I didn't mind talking to her since that meant she spent more time sitting with me.

"Why are you building your own house?"

"Because none of the contractors in this town are honest. They're just a bunch of crooked bastards."

"So that's why you were always yelling at them? I thought maybe you had anger management problems."

I laughed at that observation.

"Yeah, I can see where you'd get that impression. No, I'm only like that when someone is trying to screw me over. I'm normally a nice guy."

"Yeah, I noticed that once those guys were gone, you didn't yell at anybody."

I nodded.

"How about you, Sunshine? Why do the kids ignore you? I've seen how they never talk to you after you get off the bus."

"I'm not part of their clique. I sort of hang out with the geeks at school."

"Does that mean you are really smart?"

"Hah, I wish. No, I just prefer those guys to the rest of the kids. They aren't so picky about what I wear or the music I listen to. But I don't have to worry about that anymore."

"Why not?"

"I graduated last week."

"Oh. Okay, well, great! Congratulations!"

I felt a wave of relief shoot through me when she said that.

"Thanks."

"So, what's next? College?"

"Yeah, maybe. I don't know."

"You got good grades, right?"

"I guess. I managed to get A's and B's. Mostly B's."

"Nothing wrong with that. I remember getting a few C's and the occasional D."

She thought about that for a few moments. She tilted her head and frowned.

"What do you do for a job? I mean, why aren't you at work now? Are you taking vacation to do this?"

I smiled to myself at the change in subject.

"No. I don't really have a job. At least, not a job where I have to be somewhere to work, anyway. I work for myself. I invented a couple little gadgets that made me a bit of money."

"Cool! What'd you invent?"

"Oh, some little widget that makes a bigger widget work better."

She punched me in the arm.

"Come on! Tell me. What'd you invent?"

"It's embarrassing. Let's just say I made something for grown-ups."

"Hey, that's not fair! I'm grown up. Tell me. I really want to know."

I didn't really want to spill the beans about my inventions. Once people found out what I came up with, they tended to shun me. That was the mild reaction. More often than not, I was treated like a pariah. I didn't know if I could trust her enough not to freak out. I also didn't want word of my inventions to get around the neighborhood. Nobody had tried to tar and feather me yet, but there was always a first time for everything.

"Can you keep a secret, Sunshine?"

She frowned. After a few moments of silence she answered.

"Yes, I can keep a secret, Peter. You can trust me."

"If I tell you, you can't tell anyone else. I mean it. Especially, your parents. Most people treat me like crap after they find out what I made. I don't want to be chased out of the neighborhood before I get a chance to live in my new house."

"Whoa. It's not something bad is it?"

"No, it's not bad. It's just that a lot of people get very uncomfortable when something like that is made public."

"How come people get upset about it if it's not bad?"

"Whew. You aren't making this easy for me, Sunshine. Its adult oriented."

"Ohhhhh."

Giggling, she turned her head and gave me a sidelong glance. She was grinning, her tongue pushing against the inside of her cheek. My inner voice groaned. She was so damned cute when she did that.

"Yeah, okay. At least you didn't run screaming for home."

"You got rich from inventing something like that?"

"I wouldn't say I'm rich, but yeah, I'm not hurting for money."

She giggled again.

"So, lots of people buy your invention but shun you in public?"

I snorted.

"Yep, that's the way it works, Sunshine. People are hypocrites."

"That's messed up."

"That's just the way the world works."

"Well, that sucks."

"Sure does, Sunshine."

We stopped talking as soon as the work crew got back from their lunch. Sunshine gave me one more of those cute looks and then left giggling at my embarrassment. The guys gave me a bit of grief over that. I cured them of it, though, by threatening to make them dig a moat around the house. I didn't hear one word about her for the rest of the day.

On Friday, I brought something special. I had learned through our short discussions that she was partial to root beer. I had a small container of Ben & Jerry's Half-Baked ice cream and two bottles of Sioux City Birch Beer. Thoroughly decadent, but worth it. I also had brought along a pair of camp chairs. The really nice ones with fold out leg rest.

When Sunshine showed up right after the crew bugged out for lunch, she watched me set up the chairs. A really nice smile was on her face when I turned around to see her watching me. Of course, me being the gentleman that I am, I had to say something.

"My Lady's throne is now ready."

She giggled and blushed.

"Thank you, kind sir."

She sat down in the chair and grinned up at me. I put my feet up on the rests and opened my lunch pail. The really nice thing about Sunshine was that she never tried talking to me while I ate. Always waiting for me to finish before breaking the silence. She gave me a strange look when I brought out the tall cups and a scoop. When I opened the cooler and brought out the ice cream and the sodas, she squealed with delight. I laughed at her excitement.

She squirmed in her chair while I scooped out the ice cream and poured the Birch Beer. After placing bendable straws in each cup, I handed her one. She was smiling at me, but when she took that first sip, I swear she had an orgasm. She hummed and wiggled some more. My first thought was, I have to do this more often.

We sat on the porch and enjoyed our root beer floats. Sunshine would occasionally look over at me and hum. When we had finished our drinks, she thanked me again and left to go home. The sugar rush from the ice cream and soda hit me. I managed to get quite a bit done in spite of it being a Friday. Since I didn't want to pay for overtime, I let the rest of the crew have the weekend off.

Saturday morning I was walking around the jobsite looking over the previous week's projects and double-checking to make sure they had all been done to my satisfaction. I didn't have to correct too many things. The window installers were scheduled to come Monday and I made sure all the openings were finished and ready for the casements.

Before lunchtime, I looked out to the west and noticed that there was a line of huge billowing thunderheads building up. One had already topped out and was making the classic anvil shape that signaled a heavy storm system. The bottoms were turning blue-black and I could see the occasional flash of lightning. It was already 95 degrees and with the appearance of those storm clouds, I knew there was a possibility of hail or even a tornado.

I went over to my truck and turned on the radio to the local weather station. The National Weather Service was already issuing severe thunderstorm advisories. As I sat and listened to the updates I could feel the breeze shift directions and the distinct scent of rain and ozone wafted by. Oh shit, I thought, this is going to be bad. The temperature was dropping fast and goose bumps formed on my arms and neck.

I grabbed several tarp sections and started running towards the house. I started the air compressor and grabbed up the staple gun. I managed to cover the two skylight openings and most of the upper floor windows before the first large raindrops started to fall. The thunder had been rumbling for at least twenty minutes and was getting louder by the minute. I maneuvered the air compressor onto the front porch out of the rain and continued to staple up tarps.

The sharp pop of something hitting metal was my hint to get inside. I ran for the porch. The air hose caught on something and like a dummy, I forgot to let go. I tumbled to the ground, skinning my knees and hands. I jumped up, leaving the staple gun behind. I only got hit a couple times before getting under cover. I watched with a sinking feeling as the hailstones got bigger. In a few seconds, golf ball sized hail started falling from the black sky.

A huge bolt of lightning hit down the street, nearly blinding me. My ears were ringing from the ripping boom that filled the air.

The wind was picking up fast and I started to worry about tornados. The hail finally stopped but the heavy rain continued to fall. I could barely see across the street. It looked like a wall of white haze coming towards me as I stood on the porch. I heard a familiar voice call my name but I couldn't see her. The second time she called, I spotted her under a car about fifty yards up the street.

I ran to the truck and got my umbrella from behind the seat and ran towards her. I popped it open and she crawled out. She smiled her thanks and we both ran back to my porch. The umbrella didn't help much since the wind had really started to blow, causing the rain to come down sideways. Once on the porch we stood looking at each other for a second and then we started laughing. We were soaked to the skin and looked like we had gone swimming with our clothes on.

As we were laughing at each other, I heard the distinctive warning tones from the radio in my truck. The tornado warning sirens started going off all over town. We stopped laughing and started looking around to see if we could spot the funnel cloud. I think I was the first one to hear the low rumble coming from the northeast. I grabbed Sunshine's arm and hauled her towards the door. She squeaked in surprise.

"COME ON! We need to get to the basement right NOW! It's headed our way!"

She didn't say anything but her face was pale. She followed me as I rushed for the stairs leading down into the basement. I went over to the alcove that was meant for the hot water heater and pushed her into it. I grabbed a tarp and got inside next to her. I spread out the tarp to cover us and listened for the rumble to get louder.

The wind was howling through the window openings as the sound of a dozen jet engines got louder. I looked out the casement portal in front of me and I could see debris bouncing across the yard. It was definitely getting closer. My ears popped and Sunshine squeezed my arm tightly. She put her head against my shoulder and I put my arm around her. The sound became deafening as the twister got closer. There was a very loud grinding noise followed by a crash. Dust and small pieces of debris came flying through the window openings.

The air pressure changed and I could feel the air getting pulled from my lungs. Sunshine yelled something but I couldn't make it out. I had to pull the tarp over us completely to keep the worst of the debris from hitting us. There were more loud bangs above us but I didn't poke my head out to look. We stayed huddled together under the tarp while the storm raged above us. Finally the rumbling whine started to fade. When I could just barely hear it, I slipped the tarp off of us and stood up.

Dust still swirled in the basement but I didn't see anything flying around outside. Just a gentle rainfall was coming down now and the wind had died down to a stiff breeze. I helped Sunshine stand up and I hugged her.

"Are you okay, Sunshine?"

"Yeah. You?"

"Nothing a good shower won't fix. Let's go outside and see how bad it is."

"Okay."

When we stepped out onto the porch and looked around, I was speechless. The neighborhood looked like a war zone. My truck was gone. So was the car that Sunshine had hid under. I stepped out into the yard and surveyed the house. Other than losing the tarps I had stapled up, nothing looked damaged. I could hear the sirens from emergency vehicles all around us but I didn't see any of the flashing lights.

The cold rain felt good on the back of my neck as I stood in the middle of my yard. Sunshine grabbed my hand.

"I need to go check on my parents."

"I'll go with you in case they need help."

"Thanks Peter."

She started jogging down the sidewalk, dodging around tree branches and broken furniture. I looked ahead to make sure there weren't any downed power lines in our path. People were coming out of their houses now and looking around at the devastation. Most were standing around with a dazed look on their faces. Several of the houses had their roofs missing. Cars and trucks flipped over in the yards or the middle of the street. When we had traveled about two blocks, I found my truck. Or more accurately, what was left of my truck.

It was on its side wrapped three fourths of the way around a tree, completely destroyed. Sunshine spotted it too. She turned to look at me.

"Whoa."

"I guess I'll be shopping for a new truck next week. I don't think I'll be the only one either."

"No, I don't suppose you will be."

"Let's get to your house so we can see how your parents are doing."

She nodded and continued down the sidewalk. We went down the street another half a block and she stopped. She was looking at a pile of timbers and brick. It wasn't in the shape of a house anymore. She ran towards the pile of rubble yelling out something in Chinese.

"Mawmaw! Bawbaw! Knee mon tsai naw lee!

She was looking for a place to get into the pile of rubble but neither one of us could see an easy opening. I asked Sunshine where the basement stairs were located. I started pulling boards and other debris out of the way. A few of the neighbors saw what we were doing and came over to help.

Within a few minutes there were more than a dozen people helping us clear away broken two by fours and bricks. Sunshine continued to call out. I had tried using my cell phone to call for help but all I got was a pre-recorded message saying, "All circuits are busy. Please try your call again later."

After an hour of careful removal we found the stairwell opening and heard a faint voice coming from down below. Sunshine yelled down and they answered back. Since she was still using Chinese, I had no idea what she was saying. I held onto her shoulder and told her to stay put. I pushed the broken section of a door out of the way and managed to crawl into the stairwell. Some thoughtful soul handed me a flashlight and I started down the stairs.

I kicked aside broken bricks and glass shards from the steps as I went. I certainly didn't need to slip and bust my ass. When I got to the bottom of the stairwell, I could hear water dripping and I could smell gas. I yelled back up the stairs for everyone to clear out and not to light any candles or cigarettes. I moved past the semi-collapsed door frame, making sure not to disturb it any more than I had to. I called out to them so I could locate where they were.

I heard a groan coming from a doorway to my left and I rushed over. As I played the beam from the flashlight around, I found two people huddled inside a bathtub. Several ceiling joists had fallen over the top and they couldn't get out. I set the flashlight on top of the broken toilet, and tried moving one of the joists. It moved enough for the lady to wiggle out of the tub. The gentleman couldn't move because of a shattered wall stud, it had him pinned against the side of the tub. I turned to the woman.

"Go up the stairs, there's gas leaking and it's too dangerous to stay."

She didn't seem to understand what I was saying. I motioned for her to go up the stairs and she shook her head. I turned her towards the doorway and pushed her gently.

"Go on. I'll get him out and be right behind you."

I think she finally understood what I was trying to convey. She nodded hesitantly, and slowly made her way out. I turned back to the tub and looked around on the floor. I picked up a four-foot long section of two by four and used it to leverage the shattered stud away from him. He groaned in pain but managed to slide out from behind it. I helped him stand, careful to not pull on his arm. I could tell it was broken from the un-natural bend in his forearm.

I pulled his good arm over my shoulder and helped him walk out. The woman was waiting for us at the bottom of the stairs. As soon as she saw me helping her husband, she went up the stairs. I helped him go under the sagging doorframe and got him out of the basement as quick as I could. The smell of gas was getting stronger, and I was starting to feel the effects of exposure. Once we were at the top, Sunshine rushed up to us and took my place.

"Thanks for all the help everybody. We need to get away from here, the gas is building up down there and it might go up any second."

People started backing away quickly. I turned to Sunshine and her parents.

"Can you make it to my house?"

Sunshine translated my question to her parents. They nodded and we started heading back up the street. It took us a bit longer to get there and I had taken over helping Sunshine's father to walk. Once we were inside my house, I had Sunshine set up the camp chairs for them. They nodded gratefully to me and sat down with a sigh of relief. Luckily, I had put my cooler inside the house instead of leaving it in my truck. I got out sodas for everyone.

I assumed they were thanking me for the drinks, but I couldn't understand a word of their singsong language. Sunshine took pity on me and translated. I guessed right. I smiled and nodded.

"I'm just glad you are safe. If I have anything that will help, you are welcome to it."

They thanked me again for my generosity and the help I had given them. Sunshine said something else to them and both parents gave me a penetrating stare. I thought I had done something to offend them but they smiled when they saw my look of concern. I saw her father wince when he tried to shift in the chair. I tried to think of anything I had around the worksite that might be of any help. Since my first-aid kit had been in my truck and it was now wrapped around a tree, I didn't even have an aspirin to give him.

I heard a large truck drive by the house and I went outside to see if it was an emergency service vehicle. No such luck, it was a mobile TV news van. They had stopped about a hundred yards up the street and people were gravitating towards it like ants to sugar. The crew got out and a cameraman started filming immediately. I told Sunshine to stay with her parents and I was going to see if they had a radio so I could get help.

By the time I got to the news van, the reporter had started talking to people. One of the seven immutable laws of the universe was being enacted. The reporter had picked out the dumbest sounding hick and was asking them to describe what the tornado had looked like. I went around to the other side and found the engineer monitoring his equipment.

"Hey buddy, can you radio for an ambulance? I have a friend who has a broken arm and he needs medical attention soon."

"Yeah, just give me a minute and I'll see if I can find one that's available. I don't know how long you might have to wait, though. This town got its ass kicked today and they are short handed."

"At least make the call, please. I don't want to try and re-set his arm myself and he'll go into shock."

"Okay, I'll try."

"Thanks pal."

I stood off to the side and waited to make sure he would make the call. As soon as the reporter had his star redneck interview on tape, the engineer called for help. After several denials, he finally found a crew that could be here in about 45 minutes. He looked at me and shrugged.

"That's the best I could do."

"Hey, thanks a lot. I really appreciate it."

I jogged back to the house to relay the good news. Sunshine's father wasn't looking too good. I scrounged around and found a plastic bag. I filled it with ice from the cooler and gently placed it over the break. I hoped it would numb it a little and keep the swelling down. I had Sunshine retrieve the tarp from the basement and draped it over his shoulders. It was the best I could do at the moment. He tried to smile but it was more of a grimace. I patted him on his good shoulder and said it would be okay.

I stood out front waiting for the ambulance to show up, leaving Sunshine with her parents. It gave me a chance to think about what I had been doing and the potential for disaster. Sunshine's parents seemed like decent folks and I didn't want to make them angry by doing something foolish with their only daughter. Her father wasn't much older than me. I didn't think he would be too pleased to find out I was thinking of going beyond casual friendship with his daughter.

I was still debating with myself over what I should do when the ambulance came around the corner. I jogged down to the street and waved at them. They sped up when they spotted me. When they pulled up in front of my house, I told the driver what I needed. Him and his partner got the stretcher out and followed me into the house. They took one look at his arm and got out a sling to immobilize the arm. They got him onto the stretcher and headed out. All of us followed them to the ambulance.

They would only let one person ride in the back. There was a rapid-fire conversation between mother and daughter. Finally, her mother got into the ambulance with her husband and Sunshine was left standing next to me. Sunshine looked up at me and she was trying not to cry.

"Mother says I'm to stay with you."

"Oh. Um, okay."

There was a lot more said than that, but Sunshine wasn't telling me anything else. I looked up at her mother and our eyes locked. She didn't say anything. The driver closed the door and turned the ambulance around and headed off to the hospital. Her mother was looking at me through the rear window. I didn't look away from that gaze until the ambulance rounded the corner and was gone. Sunshine wrapped her arms around my waist and put her head against my chest. I could feel her tears soaking through my shirt. I wrapped my arm around her shoulder and stroked her hair.

"It'll be okay, Sunshine. I promise."

She nodded but didn't say anything. We stood there in the middle of the street hugging each other until we had to move for the TV crew to leave.

CHAPTER 2

Around midnight we finally made it to my apartment. It had been a very stressful and tiring walk. Twice we had to detour around downed power lines. The nicest part of the whole ordeal was being able to hold Sunshine's hand. She refused to let go. Not that I minded; I'm not that stupid.

I opened the door and pointed her towards the bathroom. She had been getting antsy for the past four blocks. I couldn't blame her. I needed to go pretty bad myself, but was too embarrassed to whip it out and piss on a tree.

Since the power was still on I checked to see if the phone service was intact. No such luck. My cellphone still gave me the message that all circuits were busy. Damn. When she came out of the bathroom I pointed to the kitchen.

"My turn. Go help yourself to whatever you find. There's sodas and juice in the fridge. If you're hungry, eat whatever you want."

Sunshine nodded and slipped past me as I headed into the bathroom. When I came back out I could hear her rummaging through the cupboards. I retrieved an air mattress from the utility closet and set it up in the living room. I had to do some creative rearranging of the furniture to make room. I could smell a hot skillet by the time I got the sheets and a pillow on the mattress.

I stood in the doorway watching her move around the kitchen. My first impression was that she looked right at home. I watched her for several moments before she was aware of my presence.

She caught me staring. I didn't think she could get any cuter, but the grin she gave me coupled with her rosy cheeks made my chest tighten. Whoa. I really liked what I saw.

"Whatcha cookin' Sunshine?"

"Grilled cheese sandwiches. Is that okay?"

"Perfect. I tried calling the hospital but the landlines are out here too and the cellphone won't go through."

"Okay, thanks for trying. Do you think we should go to the hospital after we eat?"

"I don't know, Sunshine. I'm dead-on-my-feet tired. Besides, even if I had access to my other truck tonight, I don't know if we could get to the hospital."

"Oh, yeah. We'll try in the morning, though, right?"

"Yes. If it looks like the city has cleared the roads enough, we'll try first thing after breakfast."

We ate our grilled cheese sandwiches and potato chips with a big glass of orange juice. After we were done, I showed her the mattress I had set up for her. I knew I felt grungy and wanted to take a shower. I figured she would too.

"Do you want to take a shower before going to bed?"

"Yeah, I would."

"Okay, I'll get you a towel. I'll look through my drawers to see if I have an old shirt you can use to sleep in."

"Thanks Peter."

Once she was in the shower, I dug through my t-shirt collection. I found an old Iron Maiden concert t-shirt that looked like it would be long enough. When she came out of the bathroom with her hair wet and wrapped in a towel, I was struck by how sexy she looked. She blushed all the way down to where the towel covered her chest when she saw me staring.

"Uh, sorry. Here, I found a shirt that should be okay to sleep in."

She held it up to check out the graphics.

"What's an Iron Maiden? Some satanic cult thing?"

I couldn't help but laugh. It also made me feel really old.

"No. It was a band I listened to during my rebellious youth."

"Oh. Weird."

She went back into the bathroom to change. She came back out carrying her dirty clothes and the wet towel. The t-shirt went down to her knees. Shucks. I was hoping to see more of her legs. Stop it, I told myself. I could get into way too much trouble thinking things like that. Even if Sunshine's parents gave her permission to be here; I'm sure there was nothing in that agreement that implied ogling her was permitted.

I took her dirty clothes and loaded them into the washer. I was tempted to sniff her panties, but stopped myself. Damn it man! Get a hold of yourself. Quit thinking like a pervert and act like a gentleman. I finished arguing with myself. Didn't someone tell me once that arguing with yourself was okay as long as you didn't lose? Crap! Now what?

I got a towel and a robe and took my own shower. I tried the cold-water trick. It didn't help much. I loaded my dirty clothes in with hers and started the washer. Sunshine was already under the covers and appeared to be asleep. I didn't disturb her. I crawled into my own bed and tried to think of anything except her being naked under that t-shirt.

I don't remember my dreams that night. The next morning was definitely a shock. I woke up feeling something squeezing my hard-on. It wasn't my hand, either. I could feel a warm body pressed up against my back and an arm draped over my hip. The wonderful sensation of fingers gently gripping my shaft startled me. I froze. Holy shit!

"Uh, Sunshine?"

"Yes, Peter?"

"What do you think you are doing?"

She giggled in my ear.

"What does it feel like I'm doing?"

"You shouldn't do that. It's not right. I could get into a lot of trouble."

"No you won't. I'll be eighteen next week. Besides, I want to do this. I think I love you."

OH CHRIST ON A CRUTCH! What the hell am I going to do now? Wait a minute. Isn't this what I was secretly hoping for? Hey, dumbass, wake up. She thinks she loves you. Why? What could she possibly see in me? I'm too old for her.

"Peter?"

Oh, shit. Say something asshole.

"What is it, Sunshine?"

"Do you love me?"

AWWWW SHIT! What do I say to that? You'd better answer quick or she's going to get mad and leave.

"I... uh... don't know, Sunshine. I know I am really fond of you, but I don't know if it's love yet."

"I'm okay with that. I can wait."

She squeezed my dick again and kissed the back of my neck. Alright, I admit it. What she was doing felt great. I wouldn't mind waking up to this every morning. Ooh. Parents. Hadn't thought of that yet, have you, bucko. What were they going to say about this? I suddenly remembered the expression her mother had last night. Hmmm. I think maybe she knew. How about that. Maybe I wasn't in deep kimchi after all.

"Uh, Sunshine?"

"Yeah?"

"I need to get up."

"Awww. Why?"

"I have to pee really, really bad. That's why."

"Then why are you all hard like this?"

"That's what happens to guys in the morning, Sunshine. We get 'piss hard-ons'."

"Oh. I thought it was because you were thinking about me."

It was my turn to chuckle.

"Yes, any other time of the day it would be, Sunshine. But at seven o'clock in the morning, it means I have to pee."

She let go of me and rolled onto her back. I slid out from under the covers and looked back at her. I groaned out loud this time. She raised her arms up over her head and smiled at me. A dark nipple peeked out from under the edge of the sheet. I couldn't help but stare at it. She started giggling.

"I thought you had to pee?"

I shook my head and groaned again.

"I do, damn it. But seeing you like this is tough to walk away from."

"Then go pee so you can get back into bed with me."

"Yes, your highness."

I bowed and went to the bathroom. Her giggles followed me all the way. As I stood emptying my bladder, I thought about what I was going to do next. Should I go back in there and finish what she was hinting at? I went over the conversation we just had. Something struck me as a little odd. She didn't know about 'morning wood', but yet she had had her hand wrapped around me like she knew what she was doing. The display she put on for me as I got out of bed also hinted at her knowing what she was doing.

I thought about it some more as I stood in front of the mirror looking at myself. What if she was a virgin? Oh, buddy, you will be in deep shit if she is. I can't just walk in there and ask. I might be an asshole occasionally but that would be over the line. No, I need to slow this down. I am not going to have sex with her this morning. I need to know more about her before I go that far. I haven't even kissed her yet. Well, you big dummy, get in there and do that.

I walked back into the bedroom. She had lowered the sheet to uncover both nipples. She was also biting her lower lip and her expression was unsure. Oh, yeah, Pete, you'd better slow this down before it becomes a train wreck. I stepped over to the side of the bed. Leaning over, I pulled the sheet up to her chin. I saw the confusion on her face and before she could say anything, I kissed her. A real nice, slow, gentle kiss. I stood back up.

"That's what I've wanted to do for the past week. Let's just take it easy for right now, okay? We still have to go get your parents at the hospital this morning."

I watched her expression go from bliss to a frown. She stuck out her lower lip.

"Awww. Why'd you have to bring them up? Mood kill, Pete. That wasn't nice."

"I know, but don't you think they would appreciate it if we didn't forget about them?"

"Okay. You're right. I just wanted..."

"I know what you wanted, but that's not going to happen just yet, Sunshine. I need a little bit more time before I decide I want you in my life like that."

"But, your, uh..."

She was pointing at my crotch. I laughed.

"You need to leave that alone for a while longer, Sunshine. Please?"

"Okay."

She pouted again. That chilled me out inside. Her behavior was not what I was used to. Twenty years ago, this conversation would not have gone this way. But today, it was a different matter entirely. I really needed to think with the head on my shoulders and not the one trying to poke its way out of my boxers.

I grabbed my robe and went to the kitchen to make breakfast. I turned on the TV on my way past. Of course, the news channel was covering all the damage from the storm. I fixed myself a bowl of cereal and stood in front of the TV eating. The aerial footage was sobering. They were showing the path that the tornado had ripped through town. I saw my house and what remained of those around it. Holy shit, we were damned lucky last night. I made a mental note to have a storm shelter built in the back yard.

"Shit."

I turned at hearing her say that. She was staring at the TV, her eyes tearing up. I think she just finally understood what we had gone through. I set my bowl down on the coffee table. I held my arms open and she slowly came towards me. I wrapped my arms around her and hugged her close.

"I told you last night that everything would be okay. Trust me. I'll help any way I can. Now, go get yourself some breakfast and I'll see if they fixed the phone lines last night."

She nodded and went into the kitchen. I tried the landline first. Still dead. I tried my cell next. YES! I heard the ringing tones after dialing the hospital. When it picked up, all I heard was an automated message telling me that they weren't giving out names of patients over the phone. Well, at least the cell towers were working again.

Sunshine came back out to the living room and mimicked me. She stood in front of the TV watching the talking heads babble over the carnage. The assholes were even smiling. No-conscience fuckers. Oh, well. I quit watching out of frustration. I rinsed out my bowl and went into the bedroom to get dressed.

When I came back out to the living room it suddenly dawned on me that I had forgotten to put her clothes in the dryer last night. I rectified that oversight and apologized to her.

"I'm sorry, Sunshine. I didn't mean to do that."

"That's okay, Peter. I understand. I don't mind wearing your old t-shirt, even if it does have this horrible mummy thing on the front."

I chuckled at that. No I guess you don't, I thought, as I watched her curl up on the couch. The view I got was not PG-13. I forced myself to look up into her eyes. She was blushing but the grin she had was not that of an innocent. Oh shit.

"While you wait for your clothes to get dry, I'm going to walk down to the storage warehouse and get my other truck."

"Okay. You won't be gone too long, will you?"

"Nah, maybe an hour. Okay?"

"Okay."

I grabbed the key for the warehouse from the bookcase and stepped over to the back of the couch. I leaned over and kissed her on the forehead. I got a big smile for that.

"See you in a little bit, Sunshine."

My shirt and pants were soaked with sweat from the heat and humidity. It had to be close to one hundred degrees and the humidity wasn't far from that number either. I was relieved that the warehouse wasn't any further from my apartment. I didn't think I could stand it much longer before getting inside where there was some working A/C.

I unlocked the roll-up door and went inside to get my truck. I stared at it for a moment remembering the look on the custom shop proprietor's face when I drove it into his lot. That alone made it worth it for me. 'The Look' as I call it. I smile every time I see it. The slackened jaw, the eyes wide as saucers. Then the finger pointing and elbow jabs. I can read lips too. 'Holy shit' and 'Get a load of THAT' top the list of sayings when I pass by.

This thing was the product of a splurge from my first royalty check. I spent over two hundred thousand dollars on it and it was worth every penny. It took almost two years to build and I had had a hell of a time getting it licensed. It started life as a U.S. Army

M939A2 5-ton six-wheel drive cargo truck. Now, it was a 'Peter-built' special.

I had the custom shop shoehorn a Cummins ISX 565 VG turbo diesel powerplant under the hood. I had it modified with a new computer control interface, and added a water/methanol injector system. It took three months to get the Eaton Fuller Autoshift 10-speed transmission to work correctly with the six-wheel drive axles. I had to replace the CV joints and was able to keep the front axle lock out. I took a cue from the Army, and installed ABS brakes after reading all the fatal incident reports.

I had the cab reworked so that it had an air-ride system and plush seats. It also sported a sleeper cab with an auxiliary generator to run the A/C unit on top. I had all the trim pieces chromed. You'd better believe that was a pain in the ass to have done. The grill alone set me back three grand. But what makes this monstrosity stand out the most is the custom, pearl-coat over midnight-blue silver flake, paint job. I had the rims painted to match after I got a quote from the chrome shop for those. I don't think that guy wanted to take that on, so he over-priced it.

I shook myself out of my reverie and deactivated the alarm system. I climbed into the cab and hit the glow-plug switch. She rumbled to life after a moment. The LCD display came up on the dash. All the numbers were in the green across the board. I let the engine warm up for a few minutes. I turned on the A/C, and smiled in relief when the arctic cold blast came rushing out of the vents. Pushing in the valve for the parking brake, and hearing the blast of air from under the truck; I rolled her out of the warehouse.

It only took me ten minutes to get back to the apartment. I managed to get it into my parking space. I left it running and went to go get Sunshine. When she stepped outside, she stopped in her tracks. She had 'The Look'. I laughed.

"What the hell is that thing?"

"That's my other truck."

"It's HUGE!"

"I wanted something nobody else had. That's a one of a kind custom truck."

"Damn, Peter. I guess so."

I chuckled at her reaction.

"Come on; let's go get your parents. I'm sure they are wondering where we are."

She shot me a glance and grinned.

"Worried about what they'll say?"

"I just don't need your Dad calling out the National Guard to find you."

"Ha! You mean you don't want him getting a gun and trying to shoot you."

"Well, I have to admit, that thought did cross my mind more than once this morning."

"Don't sweat it, Peter. My Mom knew where I was going to be."

I got real uncomfortable with that thought.

"Climb in. I don't want to be any later than we have to be."

She giggled.

"Chicken."

I didn't respond. I opened the door for her and helped her into the cab. I did enjoy getting up close and personal with her rear end. She noticed that fact as well. When I finally tore my eyes from her cute butt and looked up she was grinning again. I shook my head and closed the door. She is going to get me into trouble, I know it.

Once we were driving down the street, Sunshine grinned at me.

"What?"

"This thing rides a whole lot better than it looks."

I was wounded by her comment. I know my face showed it

because she giggled.

"Hey! You can get out and walk, you know."

"I'll shut up. I'm sorry if I hurt your feelings, Peter."

"I'm only half-serious about you walking. Oh, alright, I'm not mad at you for maligning my pride and joy."

"Thanks for not making me walk. Seriously, Peter, this is a nice truck. It's just so big. Why get it? I know you said you wanted a one-of-a-kind truck, but..."

"Yeah, I know. It's over the top. I guess I spent so many years looking over the fence at the rich people and all the nice stuff they had. When I got that first royalty check, I sort of went crazy. I guess this thing was my therapy. My way of showing the rest of the world that I had made it to the big time."

"Do you still feel that way?"

"No, I've learned my lesson. I don't need to show anyone how much money I have by getting outlandish things."

"That's good. Nobody likes an asshole."

I almost swerved into a parked car I was laughing so hard.

"Hey! Watch where you're going, Peter. It wasn't that funny."

"Yes, it was. I said the same thing to myself this morning. I try to say that to myself as often as I can. It keeps me humble and aware that friends are a good thing to have. When you are an asshole, you don't have many friends."

"Well, duh."

I snorted and chuckled.

"You're pushing it. I can still kick you out."

"Okay, I'll stop."

She giggled. I knew what that meant. She was done, for now. I didn't think it would be the last time she yanked my chain. I shook my head and grinned. I didn't mind at all that she had a sense of humor.

When we got close to the hospital, the amount of debris I had to drive around got less. I mentally sighed with relief. The tires on this thing weren't cheap and I didn't relish the thought of having to replace one or more of them. I had kept an eye on the inflation system. It didn't have to add air to any of the tires, so I knew I didn't have a leak.

I pulled into the crowded parking lot and the Deputy Sheriff that was directing traffic looked like he was going to have a cow when I turned the corner. I grinned as I pulled up next to him.

"Where can I park, Officer?"

"Jesus! Uh, I guess drive around back where the off-duty ambulances park. None of them are back there now."

"Thanks, Officer. Have a nice day."

"Yeah, uh, you too."

I downshifted into low so the truck wouldn't lurch while I was maneuvering in the tight spaces. When I started forward, the engine revved up higher and the distinctive whine from the turbo spooling up made the Deputy turn his head. I shrugged and grinned. I drove around back and found the parking spaces he had told me about.

I got out and went around to help Sunshine climb out of the cab. She had already opened her door, and was swinging around using the handrail to lower herself down. Just as I was reaching up to help, she slipped and fell back into my arms. I grabbed her and took a step back to keep my balance. My hands ended up in a very embarrassing position. Before I could let go, she giggled and reached around behind me and put her hands on my butt. She hummed and pulled us together.

"Yeah, that's nice, Peter. I like it when you hold me like this."

What was I going to do? Let go? No. I gave her a little squeeze and kissed the top of her head.

"I can't say that I really dislike it either."

I let my hands drop away and she turned to look up at me. I got the hint. I leaned down and kissed her. I wrapped my arms around her when she pulled me close. I was getting hard now. She felt it and rubbed her stomach against the bulge that was getting bigger by the second. I groaned into her mouth. She finally let me go and grinned up at me.

"Oh, yeah. That was really nice."

"Come on, before you get me arrested for molesting you in public."

"Spoilsport. Okay. Let's get this over with."

I followed her into the hospital. We walked into chaos. People were in the halls in wheelchairs or gurneys. The nurses and few doctors were rushing around trying to keep up. We found the admissions desk but we had to wait for what seemed like forever before the line moved. Sunshine asked for her parents and had to prove that she was related. Once the duty nurse was satisfied, we were told to go to the east wing. Evidently, that's where the staff had organized for the overflow of walking wounded.

It took us almost an hour before we found them. They were leaning close and talking animatedly. When Sunshine hollered out to them they stood up and smiled. I got that intense stare from them both. I stood back a pace from them while they hugged and cried happy tears at their reunion. Sunshine stepped back and slid her arm through mine, rubbing her shoulder into my arm. Her father offered his hand and said in very broken English.

"Thank you for help me."

"You're welcome. I'm glad I could help."

Both parents pointedly looked at where Sunshine's arm was and her proximity to my body. She lifted her chin and gave them both a challenging look.

"Tah su wo duh non pawn yo."

The look I got from them wasn't hostile but it wasn't exactly friendly either. I have no idea what Sunshine said but it was something that made her parents stop smiling. The rapid exchange of Chinese was too much for me to follow. I did get the impression they were grilling her about something. Sunshine gripped my arm tightly during the whole exchange.

Finally, Sunshine looked up to me and grinned.

"Its okay, Peter. I told them that you were my boyfriend."

"Okay. And the verdict is... ?"

"Dad won't get the shotgun if that's what you are asking."

"At least that's something. I think it's time to go. I don't like being inside a hospital more than I absolutely have to."

We led them out to my truck. That really got the conversation going. It also got me a different look from her parents. This time their expressions weren't nearly so distant. I suspected that the show of wealth in the truck had them re-evaluating how well I might be able to take care of their daughter.

I started the truck and had them wait a minute while the hot air was venting. I helped her father into the sleeper cab. Once everyone else was situated comfortably, I got us away from the 'house of pain'. The Deputy eyeballed the truck again as I drove out. I picked a different route this time, hoping to find a cleaner road. We got detoured out to the highway and I was able to open up the throttle. I glanced over at Sunshine and grinned.

"Want to see what this truck is really like?"

"Uh, sure, I guess."

"Don't worry; it rides smoother when the speed picks up."

I stepped up the water/methanol mixture using the LCD control panel. I applied a bit more throttle and the turbo spooled up. I leveled it off at sixty-five mph and the ride smoothed out. The air-ride suspension absorbed all the bumps, leaving the feeling that you were floating. I got smiles from everyone once we were cruising down the highway.

"Is anybody hungry?"

Evidently everyone understood that question because there was a chorus of voices to the affirmative. I kept going down the highway, headed for the next town. It wasn't that far of a trip and I knew from the news that the storm had left them virtually untouched. As we got closer, I posed the next obvious question.

"Where does everybody want to eat?"

Sunshine discussed it with her parents and then I got a surprise.

"Let's go to Longerman's Steakhouse."

I expected to be told to go to a Chinese restaurant, not one of the best places in the state to get a steak. I agreed with their choice completely. Once I found enough space to park the truck we went inside to get a table. The hostess showed us to our table and we ordered our drinks. I excused myself to go wash my hands. I made sure that I couldn't be seen and I went to the hostess.

"I don't want a bill coming to the table. Here's my card."

I washed my hands and went back to the table. Even with the language barrier, we had a pleasant lunch. I got my favorite, a buffalo burger cooked rare. The pure buffalo meat had a nice tangy flavor that was delicious. When everyone had finished eating and settling back in their chairs, the conversation picked back up.

I know I was the topic of the conversation by the glances I got from both parents. I tried to relax but when several people are talking about you in another language, its tough not to be self-conscious. I was looking out the front window, watching a couple guys walk over to my truck and check it out. I chuckled at their reactions. A finger in my ribs let me know I was supposed to return to the conversation.

"Peter, Ma and Ba told me that our insurance company will pay for a hotel room until the house can be rebuilt."

"That's a relief."

A tiny trace of a frown flickered at the corner of Sunshine's lips at my choice of words. I knew what she was thinking. I didn't want her to think I was trying to avoid her.

"I was hoping that there was an alternative to having all four us crammed into my tiny apartment until you get something worked out."

"You would do that? Let my parents stay with you?"

"Well... yeah. I'm not heartless, Sunshine. It wouldn't be comfortable, but I'm not about to let you or your parents sleep in a community shelter if I could help it."

At this point her parents started asking questions again. At least I assumed that's what they were doing. I think I was starting to get the tone of their language, just not the content. I got another one of those weird looks again from both of them. Both said something directly to me in Chinese but I was completely clueless as to what was said. Her father then spoke to me in his best English.

"You okay. We not... to... burden. Thank you to... offer... home."

"Thank you, Mr. Qwahaung."

Before I could say anything else, Sunshine was laughing and her father was looking at me very confused.

"Peter, Quang is my name. Li is our last name. When we say our names, the last name is said first."

"Oh. I'm sorry Mr. Li. I didn't understand that before."

"It okay. You yang gui zi. Not know."

Sunshine slapped the table and gave her father a severe scowl. Mom was laughing and Dad was grinning. My guess is that I got called a name and Sunshine was sticking up for me. Since they were smiling; I didn't figure that it was meant as an insult, at least not too much of one.

I excused myself from the table and snuck over to the hostess. I signed the receipt and added forty percent for the tip. I wasn't that stingy with my money. Besides, the meal was great and the waitress had kept everyone's drinks topped off. I went back to the table and presented my next idea.

"Let's go over to Target so you can get some clothes and anything else you need."

Mr. Li started to reach for his wallet and I waved him back.

"You are my guest. It's taken care of."

He started to argue but Sunshine convinced him that it was okay. At least I assume that's what she did. I told myself that I was going to have to learn their language if I was going to be around them more. Since Sunshine had informed them that I was her 'boyfriend', I figured it would go a long way towards being welcomed in their home if I did learn it.

I drove them to the shopping center. The trip across town was interesting to say the least. Mom and Dad Li were looking out through the side windows of the sleeper and watched people point at the truck as it rumbled by. Once we got to Target and I found an appropriately distant parking spot, we went inside. I just followed behind and let them pick the pace for this shopping trip. I knew they wouldn't appreciate my shopping methods.

I shopped liked I had a mission in life. I knew exactly what I needed and where it was located. I didn't waste any time on side trips down other isles. I much preferred shopping at Target than I did at Wal-Mart. I wasn't welcome there anymore. The managers have my photo on the wall next to the greeter with a warning not to let me in. Since I pulled my Tourette's syndrome stunt to clear an isle full of white-trash loafers, I wasn't allowed back into the store. It's okay; I got over it. The look on everyone's face when I did that was priceless.

As we were walking around the store, I would occasionally graze my fingertips along Sunshine's leg. At one point, both parents were engrossed in some lengthy discussion and Sunshine wasn't looking in my direction. I used the momentary lapse to sneak up behind her and gently blow warm breath on the back of her neck.

She grabbed the cart with white knuckles to keep from collapsing to the floor. The look of pure lust and frustration that she shot me was worth it. Her parents stopped talking when they caught her looking at me like that. They both frowned but didn't say anything. I think I managed to keep the, 'who me?' innocent expression long enough.

Once everything had been shopped over twice, we finally made it to the check out line. This was when Sunshine decided to exact her revenge. I was chuckling to myself over the latest 'Alien baby born to gay male couple' headline, when two hands grabbed my butt cheeks and squeezed hard. It was totally unexpected. Which explains my reaction. I whooped like I'd been stuck with a cattle prod. One of the green ones; not one of the wimpy yellow or blue-handled sticks.

That stopped everybody in their tracks and I was the center of attention. Sunshine was trying to hide behind a candy rack. I tried to think of something to say. Then I had it. I picked up the tabloid and started pointing at the photo on the cover.

"I know this guy! I went to school with him. He's gay? And having an alien baby?"

This seemed to get everyone's funny bone activated. I still got several strange looks, but for the most part I covered for Sunshine's act and my outburst. Her parents were not amused. Sunshine hung her head and took the berating like a trooper. I'm not sure I didn't feel the heat just standing in the periphery. Once the chastisement was done, they checked out. I was relieved not to be standing inside the store any longer.

I got more looks when the hydraulic door opened up revealing a hidden cargo area on the back of the bed. I got everything stowed and we headed back to my apartment. Mr. Li wanted Sunshine to help him call around to get a hotel room. I'm glad he still wanted one. After what happened in the store, I wasn't sure he was going to leave me alone with his daughter.

When they walked into my apartment, the first thing they both stared at was the rumpled sheets on the air-mattress in the middle of the floor. There was a short discussion between the three of them that I wasn't privy too. Once again, I swore to myself to try and learn the language. You have no idea how nerve wracking it is to know someone is discussing things about you, and not being able to understand a word of it.

Sunshine pulled out the phonebook from beneath the coffee table and they started looking for a place to stay. They did have some better luck with locating a room that was within easy walking distance of a small strip mall. I drove them over and helped them check in. I carried their stuff to the room. There was an awkward silence for a few seconds. There was a short family discussion. Finally, Sunshine looked up at me,

"Peter, I told them I was staying with you instead of them."

"Ohhhkay. Uhm, is that going to get me into hot water?"

"Only if we can both squeeze into that tiny bathtub in your apartment."

I almost choked on my tongue.

"Sunshine, I'm serious. Are your parents okay with us being together?"

"Yes, Peter, they are. I told them you turned me down this morning. I also explained why you did it. That earned you the right to date me without any grief on their part."

I wasn't sure I liked it all that much that her parents knew what happened this morning. It did go a long way towards explaining all those strange looks they gave me.

"Alright, Sunshine. If that's what the situation is, then let's leave your parents to get some rest."

We said goodnight to them and left. I just shook my head at what had transpired today. I just wanted to get back to my apartment and relax with a nice cold beer and put my feet up. Having Sunshine sit in my lap while I did that was also in my thoughts. I grinned at her as I thought this. She caught the grin and gave me one in return. We were both laughing as we got into the truck.

CHAPTER 3

When I pulled into the parking lot of my apartment complex, the property manager came rushing out of his office. I saw him waving me down. I stopped and rolled down my window.

"What do you want?"

"You can't park that thing in here. You'll have to find someplace else to leave it."

"I get two parking spaces with my unit. If I use both to park my truck, then I'm not blocking anyone else."

"I'm telling you, you can't park that here."

"I don't care what you say; it's in the lease contract that I can park whatever I want in my two spaces. The only stipulation in the lease is no junk cars. This isn't junk. If you push it, I'll call my lawyer and we'll find out who is right."

He flipped me the finger and mumbled something under his breath. He turned and went back into his office. I'm sure he was going to call the owner to make trouble. I didn't care. I knew I was right about the lease, I checked it before I signed it. I pulled forward, centering my truck in the two spaces marked as mine.

Sunshine hadn't said anything during the exchange. I shut everything down and turned to her.

"I know that came across a bit harsh but that guy has been an ass to me since day one. This isn't the first time he's tried the power-trip thing on me."

"Is he going to cause trouble for you?"

"He's going to try. I know what the lease says about vehicles allowed in the complex. There isn't anything about oversize trucks. It says no junk cars and no over-the-road commercial rigs. This isn't an OTR rig; it's a 5-ton medium truck. The plates and registration list it as a SUV. That's what any legal action will look at. With no commercial tags, they can't deny me the right to park it here."

"Okay, I understand. What about me staying with you?"

"It isn't any of his business. There isn't anything in the lease about guests."

I watched her start to say something but she stayed quiet. She nodded.

"Let's go inside before this truck turns into a hotbox."

I waited until she got out before lowering the sunscreens on the windshield. Once inside the apartment, we stood in the entryway for a moment. I wasn't sure what to do or say. Sunshine grinned and left me standing there while she went into the kitchen. She came back out with two bottles of beer. She stood next to my chair and motioned for me to sit.

Once I was comfortable, she handed me a beer and then sat in my lap. I laughed and pulled her into a more comfortable position. She had been sitting directly over my crotch and I knew it wouldn't take much before something was going to rise to the occasion. She wrapped an arm around my shoulders and leaned into me. Yeah, I like this a lot.

We sipped our beer and cuddled together in the chair. She kicked off her shoes and curled up in my lap. I flipped up the footrest and grabbed the TV remote. I found a baseball game on and left the sound down low. The teams didn't matter; I was just using it for background noise. I tried to think of what to do next. We both needed to talk about the situation.

I knew she wanted to do more than just cuddle. It was comforting that she was honoring my request from this morning about slowing down. Okay, Pete, its crunch time. You have an eighteen-year-old girl who has expressed the notion that she wants to be in your bed and possibly a lot more. She told her parents that I was her boyfriend. Damn, I hadn't been that to anyone for quite some time. Did I really want her as my girlfriend?

Yeah, I did. The more I thought about it, the more I liked the feeling that thought gave me. So, what does that mean now? I never had a girlfriend move in with me so fast, but the circumstances were a lot different now. The storm had moved that timetable up in one huge leap. Did I really mind? Well, no, I thought. What about sharing my bed? That was a tougher question to answer.

I didn't know enough about her and the relationship was too new for anything to foment in my mind. I needed to ask her some questions. I needed to find out what she wanted and expected beyond one night. I just didn't want to do or say anything to screw up a potential good thing.

I had been gazing off into space and now that I had made my decision to talk, I found myself staring into her eyes. She was watching me think. There was a bit of a frown and her forehead creased a bit. I knew she was concerned. I smiled and I could see that she relaxed when I did that. I set my beer down and wiped the condensation from my hands on my jeans. I cupped the side of her face, grazing my thumb along her cheek. That earned me a smile.

"Sunshine, I like you a lot. Actually, more than a lot, but right this second I'm not sure how much more."

"Hmmm, if you keep treating me like this, I'm going to be liking you a lot more, too."

"You told your parents that I was your boyfriend."

"Yeah. Is that a problem, Peter?"

"No, it's not. I like it that you think of me in that fashion. It makes things easier, too."

"I had to tell them. They are pretty strict and old fashioned."

"If that's the case, why did they let you stay last night and now?"

She blushed and looked down. I knew she was hiding something. At least from her reaction, it wasn't too terrible.

"I told them that if they didn't allow it, I was going to run away and stay with you anyway."

I didn't like the implications of that, but I understood. I had done something similar in my youth. I couldn't deny her the same freedom of cutting the strings from home. I wasn't angry and I told her that.

"I'm not mad, Sunshine. A little concerned, maybe. They don't think I'm coercing you do they?"

"No, that's what some of the arguments today were about. I had to convince them you weren't forcing me. You were the one who convinced them."

"Me? How? I wasn't even aware that concern had been raised."

"It was your behavior and actions, Peter. You are a nice guy and they saw that today."

Now it was my turn to blush a little. I wasn't use to this kind of scrutiny or getting compliments. I wasn't comfortable when people paid me compliments. I didn't know how to accept them gracefully. That was one social skill I was never able to acquire. What she told me sunk in. Her parents basically approved of me seeing her. It wasn't just out of necessity that she was staying with me. Whew.

She leaned down and kissed my cheek. I cupped her cheek again and pulled her in for a real kiss. It was very nice and soft. She put her beer next to mine on the coffee table. She curled up closer in my lap and we kissed again. This time there was more heat in the kiss. I could feel her nipples rubbing against my chest through her shirt. I started to wonder when she took her bra off. Then realized it didn't matter. I hugged her close and kissed her.

I used my other hand to caress her back. I lowered the one holding her cheek to her neck. I tickled her ear with my fingertips and she moaned. I continued to explore her body with my hands while we kissed. I was definitely hard and it was pushing against her butt. She wiggled a little to let me know she was aware of it. That elicited a moan from me.

She pulled back enough to break the kiss. Her breathing was so fast that she couldn't do through her nose anymore. She hugged me tight, whispering in my ear.

"Oh, Peter! Yes!"

I nibbled along her jaw until I reached her earlobe. I sucked it in, grazing it with my teeth. She moaned in my ear. I continued to nibble and lick my way down her neck. Sunshine shuddered against me. What few words she tried to say came out unintelligible. I continued to lick and suck on her neck and throat. She was squirming all over my lap. I didn't think she was going to be able to stay there for long.

I ran my hands up under her shirt. Her skin was smooth and very warm to the touch. I liked it a lot. She pulled back long enough to pull her shirt over her head and tossed it aside. She pulled up on my shirt next. I helped her getting it off of me. She hugged me close, rubbing her nipples into my chest. She giggled.

"I love the way your chest hair tickles my nipples, Peter."

More giggling from her and I had to chuckle myself at her little rhyme. When we kissed this time, I ran my tongue along her upper lip. She purred and squirmed some more. I wasn't going to be able to stay like this for much longer. My dick was fighting to escape my jeans. The pressure of her squirming over it and grinding her butt against me was driving me crazy.

I slid an arm under her legs and the other behind her back. I stood up. She squealed in surprise. Her legs wrapped around my waist. I carried her into the bedroom. I tried to lay her down on the bed but she didn't want to let me go.

"Do you want to hug me some more or would you like me to get undressed?"

She let go of my neck and lay back on the bed. She was grinning and blushing. I unlaced my boots without falling over onto my face. She helped me undo the buttons on my jeans. When I slid them down, my dick popped free and almost hit her on the chin. She gasped and then laughed. Her eyes never wavered once she saw it. I stood in front of her, letting her look as much as she wanted.

She glanced up at me and licked her lips. She started to reach for it but hesitated.

"Can I touch it?"

I could only nod. Her tiny hand wrapped around as much of it as she could. Her other hand cupped my balls.

"It's gorgeous!"

That made me smile. There had been comments made about that part of my anatomy before, but never that. Her grip tightened a little and she slowly pulled on the outer skin. A tiny drop of pre-cum formed on the tip. Her eyes widened a bit. She slowly leaned down, extending her tongue. She curled the tip of her tongue and licked it off. A tiny silver strand connected her tongue and the tip of my dick. She closed her mouth and rolled her tongue around, tasting it. She smiled and looked up at me.

"You taste wonderful, Peter. It's better than I thought it would be."

I could only stare; my voice wasn't working at this point. She leaned in again, opening her mouth. Her lips surrounded the head. The warm, wet sensation of her tongue snaking around the tip sent a shiver up my spine. When she slid her tongue under the foreskin my knees buckled. The intensity of the sensations was overloading my system. My eyes were trying to roll back in their sockets. I had to put my hand out onto her shoulder to stay standing.

I had to stop her for a moment so I could lie down on the bed. Before I could scoot back, she had reattached her mouth to my dick, resuming her sucking and licking. I was in heaven. I could feel the twinge building up. I groaned and tried to say something. My orgasm hit me fast. I felt the surge pulse up the shaft. Sunshine squeezed my balls and sucked harder. I emptied myself into her mouth. I could feel her swallowing. She was humming and purring. When my hips stopped bucking, she twirled her tongue around the tip and sat back with a huge smile.

"Oh god, that was awesome, Peter!"

All I could do was grunt and grin back. My throat was parched. I cleared my throat and tried to speak.

"I should say the same thing, Sunshine. That was very intense."

She pushed out her chest and, I swear, she looked so proud of herself at that moment. I chuckled at her reaction. I was struck by how sensual she looked kneeling on the bed. Her small frame in those tight jeans, the dark brown areola of her breasts, and the small pert nipples standing out made for an intoxicating image. She hadn't let go of me yet. She still gripped my shaft, occasionally pulling up on it to keep it semi-hard; rolling my balls loosely in her fingers.

Her manipulations squeezed out one last drop of fluid. She shifted around alongside me and leaned over to get it with her tongue. She kissed the tip lightly, sucking up the last offering. She pushed the tip of her tongue into the slit. My whole body went rigid in response. I grunted and groaned. She sat back, looking over her shoulder at me and grinned like an ornery child.

"That wasn't nice, Sunshine. Well, on second thought, that did feel pretty damned good. Just warn me next time."

She pouted at first then the ornery grin returned. I reached out to caress her back. Then I spotted her feet sticking out from under her cute butt. I lowered my hand and grazed a finger down the center of her foot. She squealed and moved away from me. Her pout was fighting with her grin.

"I think it's your turn now, Sunshine."

A brief flash of concern crossed her face. The smile returned when she figured out that I was talking about her pants. I was lightly tugging on the cuff of her pant leg. She started to undo the button on her jeans when I pushed her fingers aside.

"Let me do that, please."

She bit her bottom lip and nodded. I slowly undid the button and lowered the zipper. Pulling the flaps aside, I kissed her belly. There was a tiny trace of peach fuzz above the waistband of her underwear. I slowly tugged her jeans past her hips, leaving her underwear in place. I sat up and pulled her pants off her legs, tossing them on the floor. She scooted over a little and placed her feet on my knees. I caressed the tops of her feet as I memorized every detail of her body before me.

I could see the large wet spot in the crotch of her panties. I could smell her excitement. I leaned forward and slid my arms under her back. I pushed my fingers into her hair. It was soft and silky. I put more weight on her and slid forward to kiss her. Our tongues darted and swirled together as I massaged my fingers through her hair. I could feel the wet heat soaking through her panties into my stomach as we kissed. Her legs wrapped around me and pulled me in tighter.

I kissed her chin. I ran my tongue down her throat, stopping every couple inches to graze her skin with my teeth. I worked my way down to her breasts. I lightly kissed each nipple, making them stand out just a little more. I swirled my tongue around them, occasionally kissing them as I moved. Her hands were running through my hair, tugging and pulling my head around as I licked her skin.

She started pushing my head lower. I followed her lead and began to kiss my way down her stomach. She would occasionally bump the end of my nose when her breathing hitched. I hooked my fingers in the waistband of her panties and pulled them off. The center panel slowly reversed inside out from sticking to her. When it pulled free, I was looking at a set of flushed, ruddy brown lips; swollen with her excitement. There was very little hair to hide anything. I tossed her panties over the side of the bed.

I lowered my face into her lips and kissed them. She hissed and bucked her hips into me. I slid my hands to cup the cheeks of her butt and slid my tongue up between her lips. She let out a long low moan and her legs clamped my head tight. I moved my hands up along the back of her thighs and pushed her legs up and open. I continued to lick and nibble on her lips, slurping up her juices. Her juices were flowing out of her in rivulets. Every time I flicked the hood covering her clit, she'd clench her internal muscles and another serving would rush out.

I had to swallow often as I increased my pace. Her hips were rotating and moving around in random directions as she tried to keep her clit beneath my tongue. I could hear her breath wheezing out of her throat, small whining noises interjecting now and then. I think she tried to say my name a few time while I sucked on her lips and hood, however, it wasn't intelligible. Her hip motions became a steady twitch and her breathing became labored as she got closer to her release.

I had her just where I wanted and sucked her hood and clit into my mouth, pulling hard and lashed it back and forth rapidly. Her whole body shook, her legs pulling out of my hands. I tried to hold her down, but her whole body was twitching and a high keening noise echoed in the room. I swallowed as much of her juices as I could when she came, but there was no way to keep up with the flow. It ran down the crack of her butt onto the sheets.

I was licking her lips gently as she came back down from her orgasm and she pushed my head away from her, stuttering and gasping for me to stop.

"Oh my god Peter. Please, stop, I'm too sensitive down there."

I was grinning like a kid that just got a triple scoop of ice cream before dinner. My face was a wet, slimy mess and I loved it. I licked my lips and chin as I grinned at her. She blushed and shook her head.

"That was incredible, Pete. I've never cum that hard in my life. Wow."

"I'm glad I could make you feel that good, Sunshine. Believe me; I felt great being able to give you that much pleasure. I'm happy when you're happy."

She smiled at me and stretched out, her legs over my shoulders. I made a choking sound when her thighs scissored my neck and she giggled. I crawled up between her legs until my face was above hers. Her smile changed from funny-happy to lustful-happy as my hips met hers. I sucked in my stomach and slid my hardness up between her lips and rested it on top of her mound. There was a slight twinge of fear in her eyes as I did that but she relaxed when I pressed myself between us and leaned down to kiss her.

Our kiss was brief and she pulled back a little and scrunched up her nose. She licked her lips and got a thoughtful look on her face. I knew she tasted herself from our kiss and I waited for her to make a decision about how she felt about it. After a few moments she shrugged and rose up to kiss me again. Our tongues twisted and searched each other for several long breaths. She pulled back and scrunched up her nose again.

"It's not bad, but next time, wipe your face before kissing me. Please?"

I nodded and smirked.

"No problem, Sunshine. I'm not a fan of tasting myself after I shoot into your mouth either. I know it's mine, but I'm not into recycling."

She giggled at that and nodded.

"Yeah, same here. Thanks for understanding, Pete."

I reached over to the nightstand and pulled a couple tissues from the box and wiped my face. She grinned and hugged me with her arms and legs. Now that's a hug. I love those. They're the best and if anyone disagrees, they're an idiot and in need of serious psychological counseling.

We kissed again, her lips were thin from trying not to grin and kiss me at the same time. We laughed and giggled like kids. Well, I giggled like a kid again, she was a kid. I thought about that seriously for several minutes while trading spit with our tongues. I hadn't asked, but I could tell from the small signals she'd sent that she was a virgin. Not yet eighteen and here I was pushing old age. Yeah, okay, so forty isn't "old" but it wasn't exactly young either. I was twice her age and she wanted me. I'd never really thought of a serious relationship with someone this young.

Oh, believe me, I'd lusted after cheerleaders and the Lolita's walking around the mall; but that's all it was, idle fantasy. She presented a whole new set of problems and I wasn't sure if I was going to want to go there. Well, I was already half-way there; I was naked and between her legs in my bed. I wasn't one of those guys who screwed around and then played hooky until they got the message that I wasn't going to return their calls. I'd done that once, and felt like shit for months after I realized what an asshole I'd been. I didn't defend myself when I'd gone to apologize and she'd slapped me hard. I took my punishment like a real man and walked away.

I felt myself getting another one of those awesome hugs and looked into Sunshine's eyes. She had a tentative smile on her face and I could tell she was a little worried.

"What's the matter, Pete? Where'd you go?"

I gave her a quick kiss and hugged her back.

"I'm sorry, Sunshine, I was thinking."

"About what? You don't regret being with me, do you?"

"No, sweetheart, I don't regret being with you. I was thinking about whom I used to be and who I'm becoming because of you.

I'm worried that I'm too old for you. I don't want you to give me your precious gift and then regret it later."

Her eyes watered up and her smile disappeared. Oh no, I hate when women cry. I understand it; well, not really, but I know it happens and I just accept it. That doesn't mean I like it one bit, though.

"You are not too old for me, Peter. You are perfect for me. You have no idea how sexy you are. I've wanted you since the first day I saw you working on your house. I knew you were the one for me. Now accept your fate and let me love you."

Whoa! This was the first time I'd ever gotten my ass chewed for being sexy and wanted. I didn't know how to accept what she'd said. I looked into her eyes, and saw the worry and hurt as she thought I was going to reject her. Wake up, Pete! She loves you and wants you. What more to life is there than having a woman telling you that you're sexy and she wants you? Especially when she's a sexy little minx and you're naked between her legs. Okay, Pete, its crunch time and you'd better not fuck this up.

"Okay, Sunshine. I'll accept your love as long as you accept mine. This isn't easy, so be patient with me, okay?"

She squealed and hugged me tight, the perfect hug. She kissed my neck and was crying. She whispered; her lips against my skin.

"Thank you, Pete, you won't regret this, I promise."

I thought about her promise and how it felt to have her wrapped around me. Yeah, Pete, you made the right decision. She might be young, but she's a woman and knows what she wants. She wants you and that's enough.

I hugged her back and kissed her forehead. She looked at me and the smile on her face made it all worth it. There was genuine love in her eyes and she was happy. We kissed, forming a bond and a promise to each other to try and make this work. I felt the tension leave my body as we settled into the sheets. Well, almost all the tension, there was one part of me that hadn't really stopped being stiff. She wiggled her hips, rubbing that stiff part against her mound. The groan I let loose made her giggle.

"I want you inside me, Pete. I want you so bad right now, it's not funny. Make love to me, Pete. Please?"

Now what man in his right mind would turn down a request like that? Well, a gay guy, but they don't count. I shoved my smart-ass voice to the side and paid attention to the beautiful girl in my arms. I kissed her neck, nibbling on her skin, tasting her sweat. I inhaled her scent and reveled in it. Oh, yeah, she was sexy and I wanted her.

I kissed and licked my way to her breasts, sucking on her stiffened nipples. The crinkly skin between my lips sent shivers up my spine. I loved every little detail of her, she was perfect. I started to go lower, but she pulled on my arms and shook her head.

"You already did that. It's time for something else, Pete, I need you inside me."

I nodded without saying anything. I pulled myself up on my knees and reached down to place myself at her opening. I rubbed the head between her lips, slicking myself up with her juices. She grunted and hissed between her teeth.

"Oh, God! That feels incredible, Pete. Don't stop now."

I grinned and adjusted my arms, holding myself above her. I looked into her eyes.

"You're sure about this, Sunshine?"

"Shut up and put it inside me, Pete."

Well, no sense arguing with the pretty lady. I nodded and pushed my hips forward. I felt the barrier at her opening blocking my entry. She frowned and bit her lip as I pushed against it. I kept adding more pressure, trying to be gentle. I felt her skin part and I popped past the tight ring of her opening. She whimpered and hugged me tight. I put my lips against her neck and kissed her. I stopped pushing and held myself just inside her, waiting for her to adjust.

"You okay, Sunshine?"

"Yeah, Pete, I'm okay. It hurts, but I want this. Take me, Pete."

I suckled on her neck a little more and then started pushing into her slowly. She whimpered, but put her hands on my butt and pulled me into her. I stopped, pulled back a little and then continued to slide into her. It felt like there was a ring of muscle that was trying to cut off the blood to my dick. Her wet heat surrounded my dick, and I was fighting to not come right then and there. After several short stops, I was fully inside her. I could feel her muscles clenching me and her quiet whimpers filled my ears.

I rested fully seated into her and gazed into her eyes. There were tiny tears at the corners of her eyes as she gazed up at me. She was smiling through the pain.

"I'm so full, Pete. I feel like you tore me open. Give me a few minutes, okay?"

"Of course, sweetheart; let me know when you're ready. We have all day."

She giggled and hissed when her muscles clamped down around me even tighter. I grunted and grinned back.

"Careful sweetheart, don't rip it off at the root. I need that, you know."

She giggled some more and I almost lost it feeling those ripples gripping my dick. I closed my eyes and concentrated on not shooting off inside her. I took several deep breaths until I calmed down a little and opened my eyes. She was watching me with a little grin. She nodded and kissed me. I clenched my stomach muscles and twitched the head against her cervix. I could feel the hardened knob with the tip of my dick. I fit perfectly inside her.

I pulled back until I could feel the ring of her opening gripping the crown. She was so tight I couldn't pull all the way out. Not that I wanted to; I'm not a complete idiot. I pushed into her until I bottomed out again. Her breathing was heavy like she was running a race. The intense pressure of her grip and the look of lust on her face were too much. I rocked my hips and pumped in and out of her, slowly increasing my pace.

Her whimpering and moans matched my grunts as our hips slapped against each other. I tried to control my breathing, but it was a lost cause. I could feel the itch along the sides of my dick getting intense. I knew I wasn't going to last long. I was pumping into her faster and holding my breath. It hit me like a freight train. Flashes went off in my eyes and it felt like all my internal organs were flowing out the end of my dick. I know the entire block heard my primal scream as I unloaded into her. I could feel my brain turn to mush and flow down my spine and out my dick. I pumped squirt after squirt into her.

She screamed my name and hugged me with all her strength. I was trying to catch my breath as she clenched around my shaft. I collapsed on top of her, and she grunted. I tried to laugh but didn't have the energy or the breath. I was sucking air through my parched throat like an Olympic marathoner at the end of a race. She was biting my neck and I could tell there would be a string of hickeys there tomorrow. I couldn't have cared less.

I tried to roll off of her but she did that whole body hug, including clenching around my shaft. I was wrong before, the best hug in the world is when your lover holds onto you with EVERYTHING. Her hoarse whisper against my shoulder stopped me.

"No, I want you right where you are at. You're not going anywhere. I've got you now and I'm not letting go."

Don't argue with a lady when she's gripping your shaft so tight you think it's going tear off at the root. I chuckled and kissed her forehead.

"You're the boss, sweetheart. As long as you can breathe, I'll stay right here."

She giggled at that and clenched me again. Damn that was an

awesome sensation. I hadn't felt that in a long time and didn't want it to stop anytime soon. I did lift myself up onto my elbows so I wasn't crushing her completely. I twitched inside her and she moaned. I was grinning like the Cheshire cat. She pouted momentarily and then returned my grin with her own.

"That was wonderful, Peter. I'm complete now. I love you."

I didn't have to think on that for very long. I felt the same way.

"Yep, Sunshine; after that, you're stuck with me. That was incredible."

She grinned and wiggled her hips. I could see the pride and happiness in her eyes. I couldn't blame her one little bit. She should be proud of herself. I know I'd never come that hard before and if this was my last day on Earth, I'd die a very happy man. Well, on second thought, I'd be pissed as hell. I wanted more of this and wouldn't be happy at all not getting to do it again.

I leaned down and kissed her gently. I poured my love into that kiss and she returned it. I was happy and so was she. I knew that our relationship wouldn't be 'normal', but what in this world is? As long as she loved me and I loved her, things would work out. I knew there'd be hardships ahead, but with her at my side, it would be okay. I realized that was the ultimate truth of the universe. The world wasn't a great place, but there was happiness to be found with the right person. I felt elated and lucky as hell that I'd found the person that would make me happy and love me for who I was.

I closed my eyes and shifted so that we were lying on our sides. I felt her snuggle into my arms and we drifted off to sleep, still connected and blissfully happy.